THE ALCHEMY OF SCIENCE AND MYSTERY

STEPHANNIE TALLENT

To my family, friends, and fans, who have endlessly supported me—
thank you!!!

CONTENTS

INTRODUCTION

Over the past year, I've published a collection of short stories (or, as in the case of *KnitWitch*, a combination of stories and knitting patterns) each month.

The genres have ranged from romance (*A Snowman Made of Sand*) to fantasy (the two weird west Dinah collections, the two urban fantasy Jolene collections, *The Kaleidoscope Jaguars of the Jungles of Mexicatl*, *The Monkey's Journal*), from science fiction (*Gates of Wonder*, *The Mermaid of Ellis Prime*) to mystery/crime (*One Plus One Equals More*).

That's a lot of different types of stories!

I've collected some of my favorite stories across the board and included them in this sampler collection.

Enjoy!

FANTASY AND SCIENCE FICTION AUTHOR

STEPHANNIE
TALLENT

GRATITUDE
of the
OCEAN

and five additional stories in the
Jolene Tomberlin series

GRATITUDE OF THE OCEAN

"Gratitude of the Ocean" is the first of the Jolene stories. You learn about her love of beer, her independent streak, and her magical gifts.
And you get to meet Iggy, the sea lord, who comes to land looking like a modern day young Iggy Pop.
Jolene lives near me, in modern-day Redondo Beach, California. Think coastal Los Angeles — much, much more laidback than, say, West Los Angeles.
Read more Jolene stories in the Gratitude of the Ocean *and* The Serpent in the Shallows *collections.*

———

A RAT, brown fur glistening in the moonlight, squeaked at Jolene as she tore the POLICE LINE tape loose and ducked under the half opened, half listing roll up garage door into the remains of the burned brick and steel warehouse.

"Git," Jolene said to the rat. "I'll talk to you later."

She hoped the roll-up door wouldn't crash down upon her. Shoot, she was praying the tar paper, charred plywood and scorched girders that made up the remnants of the roof stayed up where it belonged.

At least long enough for her to do a quick search.

Slagged glassware crunched under the soles of her leather and canvas combat boots. The smell of wood fire and flame retardant snuck past the surgical mask she wore.

Her sneeze echoed against the wall opposite the entrance.

Well, if there was anyone else lurking, they knew she was here. Nothing to do about it now.

The rat scrabbled at her pants leg. She sighed and picked it up, letting it nestle under her thick blonde braid, tucked under the collar of her black denim jacket. Rats got a bad rep, but she liked the little creatures.

"Best not have fleas, hon," she said to it. Its whiskers tickled her ear as it snuffled, raising the hair on the back of her neck. Messing with her ears always did that.

The warehouse *had* housed a craft brewery, Heart's Rest Brewing, one of many breweries setting up shop in the industrial area on the north side of Torrance, where rents were cheaper and you could have a couple food trucks in the parking lot.

She'd tried it once, a month or two after it opened last fall, with reservations. She liked to sip on barrel aged beers that packed a wallop of taste and booze, and Heart's Rest primarily featured easy to quaff, uncomplicated, low ABV, alcohol by volume, ales that were barely a step up from supermarket piss.

One beer had stood out, though: their barrel aged Black Shark Diving imperial stout, rich with an unusual spicy chocolate bitterness, so strange and complex and tasty that she'd had a full pour. She'd never had anything like it before, or since. They must've been working on that for awhile, to have it ready for the first month of opening. A small sign, hand printed and nailed to the wall under the chalkboard listing the beers, the price, and the ABV, alcohol by volume, noted there were more barrel aged brews on the way.

But she'd never gone back. She'd picked up a bit of food

poisoning somewhere that day, puking her guts out all night, and irrational or not, the thought of drinking any more of their beer twisted her stomach even now.

Regardless, the space had been hipster trendy, with reclaimed wood tables and benches, and a bar that stretched halfway down one side, with a poured-concrete counter top. Games and magazines had filled a short bookcase on the opposite wall. Baskets of snacks: gourmet chicharrones, artisanal bison jerky, small batch sourdough pretzels, giving the patrons something to snack on if a food truck wasn't there. Large brewing tanks had filled the back half of the warehouse, filling the air with the rich scents of hops and yeast and malt. Steel rectangular frames with panes of old wavy glass fronted the warehouse on either side of the roll up garage door that served as the entrance.

Galen Veld, the brewer/owner, seemed like a nice guy, too. She'd met him once before he hired her, at a Rotary meeting last fall.

He'd caught her eye right off: scruffy long blond hair bound in a man bun at the nape of his neck, light blue eyes, surfer's moderately muscled build, all packaged self-consciously into a white button-down shirt and khakis she'd figured he'd bought for the meeting. She'd dragged herself there to drum up private investigation business, hating the necessity, forcing herself into black trousers with a cut three years out of date and a navy, black and cream flowered silk tank she'd bought at 90% off at Nordstrom Rack. They had chitchatted politely about beer and investigatory work.

Apparently her effort had paid off. He'd kept her card, and after the police had decided a couple days ago that the brewery caught fire by accident, from a faulty breaker, Galen hired her to find out what really happened.

Jolene had two skills passed on from her Dolly Parton-loving granny in East Texas that most private investigators lacked: the ability to communicate with animals, the little ones that lived amongst humans, what rude folks called vermin, and the Sense, the ability to see, smell or hear traces of magic. To step *down*, or *sideways*, and see what was there on the other side.

She didn't advertise either, but word got around the community. At least for those who knew about alternate realities, all the things that went bump in the night if only you could just see or hear or smell them.

Jolene scanned the scorched interior with normal human vision, stroking the rat's soft fur.

She wanted to see what the brewery looked like without the Sense, first.

The concrete bar was split into multiple pieces atop the remnants of the wooden base. The bookcase with the magazines and games was a sodden pile. Heaps of charred wood filled the space formerly occupied by the tables and benches. Moonlight streamed in through the broken front windows and the gaping hole in the roof.

Back in the far half of the brewery, in the dimness, the brewing tanks appeared scorched but intact. Jolene wondered if they could be refurbished. She bet they were expensive.

Nothing she wouldn't expect from a terrible fire.

She sighed, closed her eyes, concentrated, and went *down*.

No sight, no smell, no hearing. She couldn't even feel the weight or warmth of the rat on her shoulder.

Jolene hated this. She never felt more vulnerable during the few seconds it took to access the Sense, and she didn't do vulnerable. Despite her petite build, despite looking like a blue-eyed, blonde-haired California beach bunny, she taught women's self defense classes, had earned a black belt in Krav Maga, and could hit the red center circle of a target with a 9mm every freaking time.

Well, this was why she charged the big bucks.

When she opened her eyes, the world was different: darker, more jagged, scintillating. Darkness roiled near the brewing tanks, and the stench of rotting fish and thick brine assaulted her. A deep bass beat repeatedly kicked her in the gut; waves pounding upon the shore, ceaseless, impersonal. The little rat quivered upon her shoulder with each surge, paws entangled in her braid to help keep itself steady.

The room darkened, the chilly moonlight blocked by something, darkened til the only lights were phosphorescent flakes drifting through the air, like she'd dove into the abyssal depths.

Holy Mary Mother of God. Oh yeah, Galen was right. This was so not normal. Way more, way *deeper*, than she usually saw or felt or heard when she used the Sense.

The only reason she could think of for the perp using fire was the ocean was several miles away, too far for a tsunami or kraken to be used to destroy the brewery.

And seriously, that would be overkill and more than a bit obvious.

A slurping, slithery sound from behind the brewing tanks caused her to straighten in alarm, eyes widening to pick out anything in the darkness.

Not alone, then. At least not on this side.

The little rat had gone rigid with fear. She didn't know what the rat could sense, what he could smell or hear, but he obviously recognized a predator.

Time to go. She was paid for information, not for risking her life.

She closed her eyes. Just the darkness of her lids and flickers of light impulses from her retinas. *Up.*

The briny smell disappeared. *Up.*

The wet scraping sound came closer and closer, breaking her concentration.

Phosphorescence flickered beyond her closed eyelids. She tasted a hint of sweet rot. Felt the touch of a slimy tentacle upon her wrist. Heard the panicked squeak of the rat.

UP! Just darkness, and silence, and numbness in her nose and mouth, and her ragged breathing pulling her back to the real world.

She opened her eyes. The burned brewery, soft moonlight again streaming through the hole in the roof, was cozy in comparison to the water-logged *other* reality.

A bit of sticky slime coated the shoulder of her jacket and her braid.

The little rat was gone.

———

She slumped against the red sticky vinyl of the booth of the all-night diner, shredding a paper napkin into long strips, ignoring her cooling coffee in its chipped ceramic mug. The moon had set, and it was closer to dawn than midnight, but she had decided she had to tell Galen what she'd learned ASAP.

The man had enemies with a capital E.

He slid into the booth opposite hers, dressed in faded ripped jeans and a Russian River Brewing t-shirt. His pale blue eyes were bloodshot.

"Hon, you have some scary folks with a heapload of hurt out for you," she said. No use sugar coating the news. She told him about the darkness, the waves, and the creature. Didn't tell him about the poor little rat. None of his business.

"So, merfolk, sirens, selkies," she concluded. "Or maybe someone else, someone older. That was a lot of power washing over me."

He looked away. "I have no idea who it could be," he said.

She sighed. Liar. She closed her eyes, shifted just a little, more *sideways* than *down*, then re-opened them.

Sure enough, Galen wasn't human. Least not completely. If she'd been as smart as she thought she was, she would've checked at their first meeting. Well, maybe not at the Rotary club meeting (now wouldn't that be interesting, seeing who was who?), but a day ago, when he hired her.

That scruffy blond hair? Sleek silver, a liquid metallic cloak trailing over his shoulders and so long he could nearly sit on it. Those pale blue eyes? Gleaming like aquamarines, set into a refined tanned face, the irises formed of fractal crystals of color, the effect inhuman but gorgeous. Those surfer muscles? Well, those were the same, and still nicely encased by the t-shirt and jeans.

"What are you?" she asked. Likely Sidhe, likely noble, every girl's dream faerie prince.

"None of your business," he said. He pulled his wallet out, extracted a stack of bills. "That should cover your fee. Thank you for your help, but I no longer require your assistance." He shoved the cash across the table to her and stood up.

"Wow. I think I deserve to know if that thing, or whoever set it there to guard or whatever, is going to come after me." She squinted. The money was real, not dried up leaves disguised as legal tender.

"They shouldn't."

"Thought you didn't know who it was."

"Goodbye, Miss Tomberlin." He stood.

Jerk. Prettier than a speckled pup, but who cared. Jerk.

"Got any more of that Black Shark?" she asked. "Some bottles stored elsewhere?"

Just a hunch. Sometimes she got them, and when she did, she'd learned to follow up.

He stiffened, then left.

————

Twenty minutes later she was pulling her baby blue and rust Chevy Nova into her parking space in the underground garage for her apartment building. Parking in the South Bay was at a premium, especially if an ocean view came with the property, like her third floor condo did. Worth the extra bucks given her odd hours, to have a safe and consistent parking spot.

Brininess overwhelmed her as she exited her car into the dimly lit garage.

The stink of salt and fish wasn't unusual, given the location on the sand dune right inland and above the Redondo Beach Pier.

She loved the funkiness of the pier, with the old arcade with skee ball and vintage stand up video games, the various fish and crab restaurants, and the t-shirt and shell shops. Her favorite craft beer bar, all uncomfortable stools, rickety tables, and sticky concrete and linoleum floors, but with the draft list to end all draft lists, was down there too, tucked into the northeast corner of the u-shaped marina section.

The pier smelled a bit stale and rank, of old fried fish, cotton candy, and coconut sunscreen. Touristy, but like *Lost Boys* Santa Carla, a la Santa Cruz. 1980s. She loved that it wasn't gentrified to the point of blandness like so many beach towns.

But this stench was way more than usual, for even the hottest muggiest summer day, let alone the cool spring pre-dawn hours.

She felt the lurch and pull of an icy undertow around her feet, up her calves, reaching and grasping. She tasted bitter salt, painful on her tongue. Ocean spray slashed against her bare face. The garage was a sea cave, dank and dark and rocky. Treacherous. She touched the bit of slime on her jacket shoulder.

Still damp. That poor little rat. She shuddered and closed her eyes.

UP! UP! UP!

But she hadn't invoked the Sense.

This had come to her, seeking her, lurking in wait for her.

There was no place for her to go.

She clenched her fists, shuffled one foot back, balanced herself, poised to launch an attack, and opened her eyes.

A thin figure, at least a foot taller than her five foot six, cloaked in a murky green hooded robe that swirled like seaweed in a riptide, stood quietly just out of arm's reach in front of her. He? She? tossed back their hood, wet greenish black hair trailing over their shoulders, accentuating the fish belly paleness of their skin.

Their face was angular, cheekbones sharp as the edge of a mussel shell, with lambent eyes, orange as the Garibaldi swimming in the kelp forest. Their white skin shimmered with a soft rainbow iridescence.

Beautiful. No wonder sailors gladly drowned for creatures like this.

And more terrifying than a nest of rattlesnakes.

"You sprung my trap," they said, their voice the shusharrah of windswept sand. "Meant for the despoiler. Why?"

"The despoiler?" said Jolene. "Galen?"

"He killed my children. Used them. Their fear, their deaths." The creature shuddered, stepped closer, close enough to lean in and sniff at Jolene, a ridge of scales on either side of their flat nose lighting up like a ctenophore then fading.

"You've tasted them," they said, thin lips pulling back in a grimace, exposing rows of shark-like teeth.

Jolene held herself rigid. Show no fear, show no fear. "I didn't know. I still don't kn--"

The beer. The Black Shark. That richness she'd never tasted before, the spiciness, the complexity. No. Oh no. How sick she'd been afterwards, but how good it has tasted.

"I'm so sorry." She ducked her head down, genuinely remorseful, making herself vulnerable. Hoping this inhuman creature had more mercy than that pretty two-headed snake of a Sidhe.

A claw-tipped finger under her chin, raising her head. She met those glowing orange eyes steadfastly.

"Can you lead me to him?" the creature asked. "I erred. When I destroyed the brewery, his place of torture, I erased all traces of *him*. I had hoped he would return himself, not send a proxy. Coward."

"I just have a phone number. We met at a coffee house."

They cocked their head. "I can hire *you* to find him. That is what you do, correct? Find things?"

Jolene nodded. "One of the things. But, wait -- you can track, right? That's how you found me, from the --" she stopped herself from saying slime "--the moistness from your beast?"

"My cousin," they said stiffly.

She dug in her pocket, withdrew the stack of bills. "Can you get Galen's scent from this? He just touched it, only a few hours ago."

Those orange eyes brightened. "I can." They took the bills and inhaled deeply. "Yes. Yessss." They yanked the hood up over their head, then the garage was empty except for parked cars and Jolene. No sea cave, no undertow, no spray on her face.

Just a strand of kelp laying across the hood of her car.

She left it there. A reminder.

———

She cracked open a bottle of barrel aged Imperial stout. No chocolate, no coffee, just rich thick maltiness. Meant for sipping, but she guzzled her first glass.

Sad about the creature's children. About the little rat.

Angry at Galen, but more angry at herself, for not fully checking him out, for trusting him. Burning a building seemed like such a rotten thing to do to someone.

Obviously, there were much worse things.

She finished the bottle, all 750 mls of 18% ABV, rather than capping it for the next day, then went to bed.

She twisted herself up in sweat-damp sheets, dreaming of sharks and stingrays, Garibaldi and moray eels, dolphins and sea lions, swimming free, living their lives, then being caught and tortured, those lives cut short.

———

She decided to go to the farmer's market. It closed at 1 pm, the vendors packing up swiftly, but she would have about an hour to shop. Going to the market, then cooking a meal with fresh ingredients, grounded her.

Her granny always told her a home cooked meal could settle the heart.

Her heart desperately needed some settling.

The market was crowded, but she had her favorite vendors. Fresh asparagus, pea tendrils, radishes, all went into her bag. Some Valencia oranges, a pound of Ojai Pixie tangerines.

Her cell rang. Galen's number. She hesitated, then answered, steering herself out of the crowd, heading between two booths towards the packed parking lot.

"You bitch, what have you done?" Galen said.

He wasn't just furious. He was scared. For a moment Jolene let herself savor that fear, tasting an echo of the Black Shark Diving brew.

Then let it go.

"I gave them your blood money," she said.

"Do you know what they'll do to me?!"

"I suspect. Nothing you don't deserve, nothing worse than what you did. Better run, Galen, run so far inland that the vengeful sea can't find you."

———

Jolene dipped a spoon into the pureed asparagus soup, tasted it. Delicious. Rich and bright and earthy, all at the same time. Pure.

She dished herself out a bowl of soup, topped it with a hefty spoonful of buttery toasted breadcrumbs, then a drizzle of creme fraiche, and a pinch of chopped chives cut fresh from the pot of herbs on her balcony. Poured herself a glass of St. Bernardus Tripel. Grabbed a piece of sourdough she'd picked up at the market and a pat of salted butter for it.

Perfection.

She carted it all to her balcony to watch the sunset over the Pacific, hoping to see a green flash along the horizon.

The brininess in the air was soft, unthreatening, as the sun sank, kissing the horizon then dipping below.

And....yes! the green flash, brightening the sky for a scant second.

Her cell rang. Galen's number. Her stomach clenched. So much for a nice homemade dinner.

"Hello?"

"It is done," a soft voice like sand across the boardwalk. "Thank you, Jolene Tomberlin. My children are avenged. You have my gratitude."

"I --" she said, but they had hung up. Their gratitude. Precious, to be sure...but if Galen had kin, she was in a heap of trouble.

Maybe she should've thought of that before giving the sea creature the cash. She didn't think she would've done any different.

Nothing to do about it now. Tomorrow was another -- well, everyone knew that line.

Jolene finished her soup, enjoying the caress of sea spray on her face.

ONE PLUS ONE EQUALS MORE

and four additional crime and mystery short stories

MYSTERY & SF AUTHOR

STEPHANNIE TALLENT

THE FINAL TEST OF MARIA RAMIREZ

*Did you know you can get a job where you get to legally break
into places?
Well, sort of.
Penetration testers infiltrate and test the security of companies
that hire them for that purpose: basically, to find all the holes
in their security.
Sounds like fun, right?
Maria, in this story first published in* One Plus One Equals
More, *thinks so.
Until the job doesn't go as planned....*

———

MARIA TOOK A DEEP BREATH, wishing she hadn't left her travel mug of coffee in her Ford, and licked her lips. If her mouth was any drier it'd be like taking a face plant on the beach and inhaling hot sand.

Nerves. Just nerves.

Face down gangbangers waiting for one of their own, shot and in for emergency surgery? No problem. She'd had nerves of steel as an ER nurse.

She could do this.

Maria ran through her mental checklist: get in, get past the guard, get into the list of rooms she'd memorized. Place the tiny thumb drives in the USB ports of the computers in those rooms. Get out without getting caught.

One last step up to the double glass doors: *Diligence Whitney Federal Building*, fancy black-outlined gold letters stuck to the clear glass.

The 'Y' was peeling at the bottom, dirt caking on the exposed sticky underside.

Time for some housekeeping.

She yanked open one of the glass double doors and marched straight into the entry hall, orange plastic clipboard in hand. Her no-nonsense white sneakers squeaked against the waxed terrazzo floor tiles.

Metal detector off to her right. Bathroom doors, with an old metal box of a drinking fountain between them, to her left. A government-issue metal desk manned by with heavyset, grizzled older guard in a blue uniform shirt sat between her and the hallway beyond, leading to the banks of elevators and first floor offices.

So far everything looked just like she'd been briefed.

She'd examined the blueprints, too. She liked to be prepared. She always had a good head for spatial relations.

And a certain chutzpah.

The tap of her pen against the clipboard echoed against the nicotine-stained white plaster walls. Her nose twitched. Industrial cleaners. Still couldn't wipe out the stale scent of cigarettes, even though she bet no one had smoked inside for more than twenty years.

And...pastrami and mustard? She eyed the wadded-up brown bag on the corner of the guard's desk. Lunch. She hadn't been able to eat. Too many butterflies.

"Health Department. I'm here for an inspection." Sounded good. Authoritative.

The guard frowned at the boxy beige plastic monitor so old Maria thought the screen would sport neon green characters against a black background. He typed rapidly, then looked up.

"You're not on the list."

"*Random* inspection," Maria said. "Thought this would be a good time to do it, bother the least number of folks, since most are already done for the weekend."

She wore plain canvas khakis, a little tighter on her than she wanted to admit, and a white button down shirt, with black plastic magnetic name tag reading *Maria Morales, Dept Health* stretched over two lines. Her black canvas tote bag hung off one shoulder, the strap indenting her shirt with the weight of her keys and all the thumb drives. It would have been heavier if she'd kept her .45 in its case in there too, but she'd left that in the car.

She couldn't think of any way of smuggling it in, and didn't see why she'd need it, anyways. Even if her boss Jamie at ForgeFire Security told her to keep it with her at all times.

Her straight gray-streaked black hair was pinned up into a messy bun, and her dark brown eyes were magnified by bright red-framed reading glasses.

She looked like an inspector. She knew she did. Middle aged boring woman in a dead-end bureaucratic job.

And she'd chosen today, Good Friday, for her run, because the staff would be limited at the courthouse; and after lunch, because by then, there'd hardly be anyone left at all. Good Friday might not be a federal holiday, but most businesses that kept banker's hours would be shutting down early.

Come on, man.

"I need to call—"

"Then it's not really a random inspection, is it?" Maria asked, stretching up to her full five foot six and leaning just slightly towards the guard, close enough to read his nametag. "*Harold.* And then I have to come back at some time in the future, Harold, and we go through this whole song and dance again."

"What department are you from again?" Harold the guard asked. "Seems like a busy day for inspections."

Maria tapped her nametag. "Department of Health."

"Got any other i.d.?"

¡Dios mío! Of course she'd get someone suspicious. What was Harold, a retired detective? All contract security officers had to have some law enforcement training. Just her luck she didn't get some wet behind the ears kid. She fished out a wallet out of her back pocket, pulled out both a Department of Health i.d. card and business card, and handed them to him.

"There. Happy, Harold?" she asked. "Are you going to let me do my job now?"

Harold the guard examined the card, front and back, then handed it back, along with a lanyard with a laminated orange tag labeled VISITOR OFFICIAL BUSINESS. "Have a good day, Mrs Morales. Through the hallway behind me. Cafeteria is on the second floor, but it's already shut down for the day."

"I've been here before," Maria said. "I know my way around." Granted, that was for one miserable day of jury duty, but Harold didn't have to know that.

Act like you belonged. Act with authority. Jamie had stressed that, time and again.

Easy peasy. She'd run an inner-city ER as a senior nurse before retiring from nursing. This was a piece of cake. She handed her tote and clipboard to Harold (who barely glanced at both) then stepped through the metal detector.

Shoot, maybe she could've gotten the gun in.

"Good to go?" she asked, reaching for her bag and clipboard. "Have a great day, Harold."

"You too, Mrs Morales. Happy Easter."

Maria strode down the hallway, swapping out her *Dept Health* nametag for one that said *Computer Services*. She was in.

Room 110, the office of Assistant District Attorney Sara Roberts, just past the elevators, was her first target.

That name rang a bell, but she couldn't quite place it. She'd been spending more time learning everything Jamie had thrown at her. And then, even though she was on the physical security team, on her own, learning as much as she could about the other divisions in the company. The cyber hacking stuff.

And she had a knack for that, too.

Not important. She had to focus on placing the thumb drives, each preloaded with software that would hack into the hard drives of each individual computer, then migrate out to the main servers. All she had to do was stick them in and kaboom! She earned her paycheck.

Maria jiggled the doorknob on the door to Room 110. Locked. She squinted through the vintage chicken-wire glass. Couldn't see a damn thing. She knocked firmly, rattling the glass. No answer.

She sighed, then looked around. The hallway was empty, and Harold the guard was seated looking out over the reception area, not looking down the hallway.

Her tote bag had other goodies besides the thumb drives. Maria reached in for her fuzzy bunny's foot key fob with a series of bump keys, her car remote, and her apartment key. She angled her body so that Harold, even if he did look over his shoulder, couldn't see what she was doing, then inserted one of the bump keys into the lock and smacked it with her hairbrush.

The dull thud echoed down the hallway, but Harold didn't even look up.

And just like that, the doorknob turned.

Maria had been appalled when she learned of bump keys. After practicing on the lock on her own apartment front door until she could bump it as fast as just unlocking it, she'd swapped her lock out for a more secure lock, at her own cost.

She bet the courthouse would be installing new locks on the doors after her visit.

She slipped into the quiet office, closing and locking the door behind her. As expected, the office consisted of two rooms: a front area, with a scuffed oak receptionist's desk, and a back room, the door to it shut. The white plaster walls were adorned with artwork left over from the 1970s, bold graphic prints in avocado and gold that fought against the 1920s architecture of the courthouse and the terrazzo tile that extended into the office.

Maria remembered from the blueprints that the back room would have windows overlooking the grass and bushes outside the building. Indeed, a soft afternoon glow lit up the vintage glass of the door leading to the back office.

She turned the knob (unlocked, obviously counting on security of the first door), but didn't open it.

Something felt wrong.

Like she wasn't alone.

And that smell. She knew it from the ER.

She couldn't hear anyone's breath, or even the tiny rustle of clothing, but her instincts were on full alert.

There. The shuffle of steps. The groan of an opening vintage window, then the slam of it shut.

Danger, Will Robinson!

If she didn't open the door, she failed before she even started, and her job as a penetration tester for ForgeFire Security was done. Kaput. Dead.

And Maria wasn't a quitter. She'd raised two kids by herself and put both of them through college, then survived losing both of them in a car crash, all the while working as a nurse til her knees and her back and her soul just couldn't take it.

And learned how to bump locks, after that. Threw herself through crazy obstacle courses. Learned a half dozen ways to kill someone with her bare hands.

Well, maybe not the latter. But she *had* tackled a whole new profession.

She opened the door.

And stifled a scream.

———

Either Sara Roberts hadn't cared about Easter or she had been a workaholic or both, because she was at her desk.

But Roberts wasn't working.

Roberts was dead, dead, dead, a small charred bullet hole centered on her forehead and oh, god, what a mess on the wall behind her, the afternoon light from the flanking windows just putting everything into sharp relief.

Between the nicotine-stained walls in the entry hall and the blood and brain spatter here, the whole damn courthouse needed several coats of paint.

And obviously way better physical security. Who'd Harold let in? An "electrician"? Some other "inspector"? *Busy day for inspectors, huh?*

She stepped up to the desk, hands clasped behind her back, tote bag pushed back so it wouldn't bump forward, to peer at the wound.

Yep. Probably a .45. She'd seen too many wounds like this over the years. So many the smell of gunpowder, urine, and feces smelled like the home that was the ER on a bad night.

A home she'd ran away from as soon as she was able.

A .45. Just like the one Jamie had tried to get her to bring in, but she'd decided against, knowing she had to get past security and the metal detectors. She hadn't trusted coming up with a good story to get out of her bag being looked into.

She had to get out of here. Screw the job.

Maria didn't know if this will all coincidence, her coming in and poor Sara Roberts getting killed at the same time, but she wasn't sticking around.

And besides, her work was unnecessary.

If someone could get in and murder an ADA, then obviously the security sucked.

She backed away from the desk, fishing around for the pack of hand wipes in her tote. She wiped off the doorknob, both inside and out, and tiptoed past the receptionist desk. She was reaching for the doorknob to the hallway when she saw it turn.

"Ms Roberts?" Harold. "Ms Roberts, I got a strange call. I know you said you had a lot of work and to not pester you, but I'm coming in." Keys jangled.

Fuck. Fuckety fuck.

Well, all that time in the gym and doing that damn obstacle course was now useful.

Back to Roberts' office, shutting and locking the inner door. Ignore the dead lady.

The window to the left was locked. Skip it. She'd go out the same window as the murderer. At least she knew that one opened.

The sash-and-pulley windows were likely original to the courthouse and just as slow and crotchety as she guessed she would be at the same age. Assuming she made it that long.

She shoved up on both panes, the windowpanes groaning, and squeezed out and let herself fall the four feet down.

Into the rose bushes.

The very, very thorny rose bushes.

Her visitor's tag snagged on one branch. She yanked it off and put it into her tote as she stood up. Her ankle hurt, her face stung, and one palm still had a rose thorn embedded in it.

"Ms Roberts! Oh my god!" Harold's voice, loud enough she thought he was looking down at Maria from the open window.

Maria sprinted.

But not quick enough.

"Mrs Morales! You get back here!"

Maria kept running.

———

Maria had parked her car, a nondescript five-year-old Ford, around the corner from the courthouse, on a eucalyptus-lined street with boxy 1950s houses. She hadn't wanted to mess with the courthouse parking lot with its metered parking and barriers and tickets, even though Jamie had given her a pre-paid parking lot ticket.

Thank god she hadn't.

As soon as she reached her car she scrambled in and went to work.

She unpinned her hair and fluffed it over her shoulders. She took off her red-framed readers and replaced them with aviator sunglasses. Next she pulled off her white button down shirt and balled it up and put it in her tote. Under her shirt she'd worn a tight army green cotton camisole. The day before she'd applied bright floral temporary tattoos, daisies and lilies and zinnias, on both shoulders. The colors gleamed in the afternoon sunlight; they wouldn't really start fading for another few days.

Finally, she swiped on some bright red lipstick.

Not much she could do about the khakis, but if she was driving, and all anyone could see was her head and chest, she looked different enough. She swapped out her utilitarian sneakers for beaded leather flip flops, just in case she had to get out of the car. Her toenails were painted a rich sparkly red—*The Witch's Ruby Slippers*, according to the label.

Maria didn't know if she looked particularly hip, or only like someone too old trying, but she didn't think she looked like a health inspector anymore.

Two patrol cars, lights flashing, screeched past her. One slowed long enough for the cop in the passenger side to take a quick look at her, then it continued to the courthouse.

Maria drove off.

———

Maria didn't head home, to her apartment in Redondo Beach, though that was only about four miles from the courthouse.

She might never go back there.

And she wasn't sure about going to ForgeFire. In fact, she was positive she didn't want to go there.

She turned down Western, towards the 405 freeway. She needed to find a Starbucks or something where she could do some research online.

She'd just gotten onto the northbound ramp when her company cell phone, resting on the dash, buzzed.

She looked at the screen. Jamie.

Fuck. She didn't want to answer it. Didn't want to think, even now, that he might be tracking her with this phone...equipment from ForgeFire.

She lowered the car window and flung it into the weeds next to the on ramp, just missing a homeless man in faded camo pants and a black hoodie. "Sorry, man!"

There was a Starbucks in Westchester. Barely ten miles away but it seemed like more, the other side of LAX. The airport always seemed like a dividing wall along the Santa Monica Bay.

She left the keys in the center console cupholder and put her tote bag in the trunk next to the case holding the .45. She grabbed her messenger bag and personal laptop instead.

ForgeFire had given her a laptop, just like they'd given her a phone. One of the cyber guys explained all the different systems and hardware to her.

This laptop *wasn't* that one.

This was *hers*, purchased with money saved from her first three or four paychecks at ForgeFire (paid training, one of the reasons she'd gone with ForgeFire instead one of their competitors). It was loaded with all the same sorts of software, that she'd purchased on her own. She'd never taken in to ForgeFire for help from one of the guys, not even when she wanted to throw the damn laptop against the wall when she couldn't get things loaded correctly. She'd forced herself to learn it all.

It wasn't paranoia when they might someday be out to get ya, right? The more they'd taught her at ForgeFire, the more cautious she'd become.

Maria pulled out her own personal cell phone and placed a mobile order. The less people she interacted with right now, the better.

The Starbucks was nearly empty, just a few people scattered around drinking lattes or munching on egg bites in between working on their own computers. She picked a table near the bathrooms—and a back exit. She hot-spotted off her phone and ran a search on Sara Roberts while sipping on her mocha. The caffeine settled her nerves.

It didn't take long to figure out why someone would want Sara Roberts dead. Roberts was involved in the prosecution of Mica Cambridge for running an online fraud and embezzlement scheme— to the tune of millions of dollars.

No wonder Roberts' name sounded familiar.

And Cambridge. Who Maria had met when she first got hired by ForgeFire.

"Hey, Maria, I'd like you to meet my pal Mica," Jamie had said. "Mica, meet Maria Ramirez, one of our most promising new physical security hires. Look at her. She could get in anywhere."

Both men had stepped back, assessing her. Maria knew what they saw: a Latinx woman in her early fifties, dark hair streaked with gray, newly bulked up muscles hidden under a layer of middle age spread. Fine even features in a light brown face: a fading prettiness more forgettable than nondescript.

All of that an *asset*, not a detriment.

Jesus, Maria, how could you be so stupid? She'd been so proud of herself for mastering all the skills required. So proud for studying the blueprints of the federal building for this first real job, she hadn't even thought of the people inside.

Luckily, she had a backup plan. Not just for this job.

For the whole thing. Just in case.

She typed furiously on her keyboard. Then hit return.

Five minutes, and a car marked as an Uber would come get her. And Maria Ramirez—with over two million dollars of ForgeFire's money—would disappear.

Her phone—her phone, her private phone—rang the James Bond theme.

Jamie.

She answered. Four minutes. "Hi, Jamie."

"Maria, honey, what happened? I tried to get you on the phone and it went to voicemail. What's one of the first things I taught you? Never go silent on us. I heard what happened with Roberts. You got out okay, right?"

"I got out fine, Jamie. Just fine." Three minutes.

"Babe, we need you back at the ranch. Are you holding up okay? Need me to send you a car? I know it can be a real shock, finding a dead body."

"I'm doing fine, Jamie. I've seen my share of dead people, don't you worry." Two minutes. She glanced out the front window. Navy blue Xterra, her contact had said. A CRV drove by. A Forester. And there. She couldn't see through the tinted windows to see the driver, and the angle was wrong to catch the license plate, but how many Xterras were still being driven around?

"Maria. Seriously. Where are you?"

"Jamie, I gotta run. Catch you later, okay?" Maria tapped the hang up icon, then clicked through the steps to reset and erase her phone. She stood and powered down her computer, slid it into the messenger bag.

Maria exited the Starbucks and got into the Xterra.

She'd left the phone on her chair. Maybe one of the baristas would find it. Or another customer. Someone could use it. Treasure it. Not make assumptions.

It was an old model, but it was still useful.
Still had a bit of kick to it.
And a certain chutzpah.

a SNOWMAN made of SAND

and six other sweet romance short stories

Stephannie Tallent

A SNOWMAN MADE OF SAND

I never thought I'd have fun writing sweet romances.
But I do.
There's something about knowing that you get your happily ever after,
that, in these times, is especially comforting.
Plus, I get to have fun "meeting" smart, interesting women and the
men who deserve & respect them.
I hope you enjoy meeting engineer Eliza and hot surfer/coffee house
owner Jake!

———

NO MATTER how many tree lighting ceremonies on various small town Southern Californian piers and plazas, no matter how loud the Christmas music in the upscale outdoor mall up on the hill in Palos Verdes, or how pungent the piped-in scent of pine trees it seemed was *everywhere*, it just didn't feel like Christmas to Eliza.

Maybe it was the sun glittering on the blue Pacific waves dotted with surfers in sleek black wetsuits, or the sunny, balmy seventy-degree weather, or the tourists still wading into the surf in flip flops and cargo shorts, squealing at the cold bite of the water as the waves slapped at their shins.

Or maybe, it was just that Los Angeles wasn't home.

Five months ago, she'd taken the job at Orbital Unlimited. She'd turned down Boeing, Northrop, even SpaceX, for the job. It had sounded like a dream come true, the potential to have her own team within a year. Everything she'd worked so hard for, graduating near the top of her class at Yale with a joint degree in Astrophysics and Computer Science, then to MIT for her doctorate.

All the long nights and early mornings in New Haven. All the skipped romances and parties and things that made college, well, college, even if it was a top notch school chock full of ambitious students.

The car wreck, taking away her parents right before grad school, also took away any reason to go back to Saint Charles, Illinois, where they'd moved after Eliza finished high school. She'd so loved visiting them at Christmas, window shopping in the quaint downtown area, hiking together along the Fox River in snow boots and a parka. Playing board games, from Scrabble to Catan, plus whatever special new games her dad found, pouring over online review sites.

Then, all the lonely Christmas breaks these past four years, with days and nights spent in the Barker Library at MIT at a table under its big dome, sunlight or moonlight shining through the center oculus, backlit columns aligned along the walls, studying, researching.

She would steal just a few moments at midnight for herself, tromping through fresh fallen powder, *shusharrah* squeaks under her waterproof, rubber soled boots, crisp air tight in her lungs. She always loved her solitary winter walks from the neoclassical library to her un-renovated, shabby brownstone apartment. On those nights, she didn't even mind climbing up the three flights of creaking stairs to her top floor studio, or the building's temperamental furnace. She would just curl up under her down comforter, falling asleep to the soft glow of lights on her little Christmas tree.

By morning the snowfall would be packed and gray, if not more suspicious colors, but she loved the fresh snow.

Her building had a tiny backyard, just a dirt lot filled with weeds in the summertime. Every year at Christmas break, after enough snow had accumulated and buried all the dried weeds, she'd make a small snowman, just for herself.

That last fall, when the leaves turned bright vibrant orange and scarlet and yellow, she'd started interviewing at different aerospace companies. Her advisor, Dr Lacey Jacobs, encouraged her to do a post doc, with an eye towards academia, but Eliza wanted to do hands-on, practical research and projects.

All the aerospace companies were eager to hire talented women; Orbits Unlimited more so than the others.

The company romanced her with the South Bay Los Angeles techie version of wining and dining. Mark from HR and some of the other guys took her out to local breweries featuring Hazy IPAs, fruit infused Saisons, and barrel aged Imperial stouts, with names that cleverly referenced physics and engineering. They introduced her to restaurants in nearby trendy Manhattan Beach, feeding her pasta with rich roasted bone marrow at one restaurant, flaky cheddar bacon biscuits at another, and more takes on sushi than she knew what to think of.

She was so overwhelmed and excited she didn't even notice she'd be the only female engineer, and what that said about the culture at Orbital, and why they were so eager to hire a woman.

That winter, her backyard snowman sported a blue and orange striped plywood surfboard and dark sunglasses.

———

And here she was, leaning against the salt-stained wooden railing at the end of the Hermosa Beach pier, a wary eye out for the weekend fishermen casting off the pier all around her, her long curly red hair whipping around her face in the stiff breeze. She inhaled the briny air, tasting the saltiness over her cinnamon flavored lip balm, watching the sun glitter off the ocean.

In December. Wearing saddle tanned strappy sandals, white t-shirt knotted at her flat belly, and faded cut off jeans, and reeking of coconut sunscreen. In *December*.

Two weekends ago she'd learned her fair skin would burn bright red even in the low winter sunlight: the joys of being a redhead of Irish descent.

She caught a glimpse of one rounded dorsal fin rolling in and out of the water, then another, then one more, just thirty yards away. A pod of dolphins! She smiled. So sleek and fast and free. Seeing dolphins always raised her spirits.

But then she thought of work again. Of being shut out of the big contracts. Once Orbital got her, and she had uprooted herself from the East Coast, it was like they had no clue what to do with her.

Treat her the same as the men, darn it!

Dr Jacobs had tried to warn her of the bro culture at so many of the tech firms. She hadn't had the opportunity to form any friendships here; after work, her unmarried peers took off in groups to those same breweries, ignoring her, and the rare married ones went home straight away to their wives (totally understandable).

Most of the secretaries and receptionists, almost all women, viewed her with suspicion. She wasn't one of them. She was an engineer.

She'd overheard too many snide comments from the guys about her being hired as the token female engineer (but at least hot). She'd walked into too many meetings, expecting the discussion to be about the project, and interrupted crude jokes that trailed off at her entrance, and started up when she left.

Management kept shuttling her from minor project to minor project, so she never had a chance to follow through on any of her ideas, or to even gain any support from her fellow engineers. She wasn't incompetent, but that was how she was beginning to feel.

High cirrus clouds began scudding across the sun, graying out the sky and dropping the temperature ten degrees. Eliza shivered. Sometimes it did feel like winter, even in Los Angeles.

———

Coffee. Coffee and caffeine always helped.

She'd noticed a new coffeehouse, Bean and Board, up the street from the pier, in a renovated single-story wood-sided beach cottage.

She decided to try it. She'd walk right by it on the way to her car, anyways.

The cottage had been painted a bright cheery yellow with white trim. The scent of cinnamon coffee cake and rich dark coffee wafted out of the wedged-open front door.

Her stomach growled. She loved cinnamon on anything.

She went in. The space was wide open; obviously some walls had been knocked down during the renovation. The oak floors looked original, a bit warped and beat up, but were polished to a soft warm glow. Hung on the white-painted shiplap walls were vintage longboards, some waxed to warm yellow wooden tones, others coated with bright resins, mint green and sky blue and warm red. Colorful Christmas lights festooned each longboard, reflections twinkling off the soft sheen of the boards. Photos of surfers, flat white picture frames setting off the blues of the waves and the colorful fiberglass-sheathed shortboards, were interspersed between the longboards.

A thickly cushioned cream canvas futon with red and white striped pillows sat against the back wall, its flat, unfinished pine arms broad enough to serve as end tables for a small plate with a cookie or for a mug of coffee. Knock off lacquered bent plywood Eames-style chairs around bistro tables made of recycled surfboards filled the center of the room. Several were taken by patrons, sipping espresso and munching on pastries, working on their Macs. A long, reclaimed-wood table, big enough to seat at least sixteen, was along the wall to her left. Backless benches provided seating for it.

To her right was a black laminate counter with a sleek tablet terminal as a register and a glass case full of pastries (including the coffee cake!). A sleek Italian espresso machine stretched across a second counter against the wall, along with a heavy duty grinder.

Above the espresso machine was a chalkboard menu: coffee drinks, pastries, even sandwiches. The mozzarella and heirloom tomato sandwich sounded tasty.

"What can I get you?" the barista asked.

Eliza looked up. And up. *You!* she thought. She could feel her face flush beet red.

He was tanned, with sun-streaked brown hair pulled back in a short pony tail. Broad shoulders filled a faded blue Billabong-emblazoned t-shirt, and baggy khaki shorts managed somehow to accentuate his trim waist. The bottom of a tattoo peeked out from beneath his right sleeve. And tall! Eliza was short at 5′2″, but he was at least a foot taller.

He was maybe a few years older than her, in his early thirties. Small crinkles at the corners of his eyes spoke to lots of time in the sun and water. He looked a little like a young Sam Shepherd. *The Right Stuff* was one of her favorite movies *ever*.

And those eyes ... she could fall into his gorgeous bright brown eyes forever.

They were the improbable color of cinnamon.

Cinnamon.

She was surrounded by guys at work, and not one had affected her this way, even before she realized most were jerks.

"Um," she said, then rallied. "A latte? Two shots, whole milk? And a piece of that coffee cake?"

"For here, or to go?" His voice was as rich and tasty as cinnamon, too.

"To go," she squeaked.

"Want that cake warmed up?"

Oh boy did she ever. "Yes, please." She tried to pull herself together, to say something intelligent. "How long have you guys been open?"

"Just a week since last Sunday. Crazy time of the year to open, I know, but the property became available a couple months ago and I didn't want to risk losing it. Jake," he said, sticking his hand out across the counter.

"Eliza." His grip was warm and strong; not enough to hurt, but enough to show her he respected her. Or at least that's how she interpreted it. "The place looks great. I bet you'll do great."

"Thanks," he said. "Hope so. Here's a frequent flyer card. Buy ten drinks, get the next one free." He punched the card, smiled at her, then did nine more punches. "Just want to make sure you come back." He handed it back to her, his fingers brushing hers. No rings.

Engineers do *not* swoon in coffee shops.

She fidgeted while he made her latte and warmed up the cake, looking everywhere but at him. Except for sidelong glances she couldn't help.

He placed her items on the counter. "Sugar, cocoa powder, napkins etc are over there." Jake gestured to a table off to the side, set up with various coffee accoutrements. "Hey, I don't know if you like board games, but I'm hosting—well, the coffee shop is—game nights on Tuesdays. You should come. 7 p.m. Redeem that free latte."

"Thanks," Eliza said. "I will."

———

Jake watched the young woman leave. Cute as a button, with all that curly red hair and bright green eyes. A little awkward, but sweet. He really hoped she'd come back on Tuesday. His sister Kathy would be running the counter, freeing him up to have some fun playing board games. He'd barely had any time off for the last couple months, getting Bean and Board up and running.

And it'd been longer than that since he'd met a girl he wanted to see more than once. Since that nasty break up with Ashley.

Yes, he was looking forward to Tuesday night.

———

Monday morning, back to work. Eliza carefully parked her cherry red Miata, a gift to herself for landing the Orbital job, in the corner of the lot furthest from the entrance. So far it didn't have any dings, and she wanted to keep it that way.

Orbital Unlimited, headquartered in El Segundo, just south of the Los Angeles airport, operated out of a newly built modern building. Constructed of thick concrete slabs and immense glass panes, the building sprawled, taking up half the city block. The interior was half computer and other laboratories, half office space and conference rooms. It did have a coffee bar and lounge downstairs, along with old-school stand up video arcade games like Galaga and Pac-Man, for when the teams needed a break.

"Hi, Shelly," Eliza greeted the receptionist, who was typing away at her keyboard at her sleek curved desk in the terrazzo-floored entryway.

Shelly glanced up, pushing her thick, blond-streaked hair out of her sharp featured, tanned face. "Message from the boss," she said. "Mike wants to see you as soon you get in." She went back to typing.

Eliza stood still, unsure. Did that mean after she at least dropped off her messenger bag at her desk?

"Now," said Shelly, not even looking up. "He's in his office."

Eliza went straight there, mind buzzing in worry. She had double checked all her numbers and coding on the last simulation, checking re-entry stability for a prototype sub-orbital small passenger ship.

She knew she hadn't made any mistakes. Her work was nearly always perfect, to the grudging acknowledgement of the other engineers.

"Come in," Mike said as she knocked on the doorframe to his glassed-in office. He was reviewing reports at his desk, a teak and steel Mad Men monstrosity. Two Herman Miller ivory leather office chairs sat in front of the desk. From the full length windows behind it he had a peek view of the tree-filled acreage of the adjacent refinery after which the town was named: El Segundo, The Second, location of the second Standard Oil refinery in California.

Mike was older that most of the engineers; even so, she gauged him to be in his early 40s, not any older, with a round, clean shaven face, cold blue eyes, and dark hair just starting to thin on top. She was a little nervous around him. He was one of the cofounders of the company.

He didn't offer for her to sit.

Or mince words.

"Eliza, we're letting you go. It's just not working out. We've tried you with different teams, and the guys just say you don't gel with any of them. It's not your work, just the team aspect. Mark from HR has a severance package for you, so go see him next. No hard feelings." He nodded to her, dismissing her, looking back down at the reports.

She stood there, stunned, her face warming to that beet red color she just couldn't suppress. *She* didn't gel? She didn't even have the chance! "Sir, respectfully, your guys shut me out of everything and ignored all my suggestions. No one would even leave me with one team long enough for me to become part of it."

He glanced up. "Perhaps," he said, "if you'd been more forceful earlier, things may've been different."

"You're blaming *me*?" She couldn't even. The gall. The unfairness. She turned and walked out, kicking aside the door stop wedging open his door and grabbing the edge of the glass door just so she could slam it. She'd show him forceful.

Going to HR would mean walking through the open office space on the second floor. If Shelly, a vicious gossip behind that sleek snooty exterior, knew Eliza was being fired, everyone else did too.

Screw them. She had to collect her things, anyways. Not that she kept much at the office that was personal.

No one met her eyes as she packed up, or as she signed paperwork with Mark in HR, or as she stomped out past Shelly, who openly gawked as her. *Screw* them.

Merry freakin' Christmas.

She peeled out of the parking lot and drove home.

———

Home was a small 1920s Spanish bungalow she rented in South Redondo Beach on an alphabet street: Avenue E, to be precise, with a sneak peek of the Pacific from her front deck. The front yard was landscaped with native plants, from aromatic sages that, when damp with dew or fog or rain, perfumed the morning air with their wild scent, to *Ceanothus* with glossy green leaves and, when in bloom, vibrant lilac flowers. Fruit trees, Eureka and Meyer lemons, Key and Persian limes, shaded the small fenced backyard, with its gravel-covered ground and fairy lights twinkling off the back deck.

She'd love to buy a home like it someday, creaking original floors and banged up plaster and all. Maybe even *this* home. Get a dog. Something soft and fluffy with floppy ears, that would curl up with her on the couch and cuddle.

She could use some cuddling right now.

Her thoughts flashed to Jake at the coffee shop.

Nope, not now. Focus on getting out a resume. The severance package was very generous, enough that she wondered if she might've had a sexual harassment case. All those crude jokes. Regardless, she had enough money, between the severance and savings, to not rush into another bad fit. But it didn't mean she could put off a job search for months, either.

She tweaked her resume, then emailed Dr Jacobs. She wanted to call, but she knew it was Christmas break at MIT.

Yes. It *was* Christmas time. And as hurt and furious as she was, maybe losing this job, that she hated anyways, was a gift. Of sorts.

She hadn't even felt up to getting a tree. Even in Boston she'd always put up a table-top sized tree, and decorated it with ornaments she'd inherited from her parents. Those ornaments were neatly packed up in boxes on the top shelf in the closet of the spare bedroom.

This year, she hadn't wanted to get a tree. Now she did, darn it. She tossed an old sheet into her car, put the top down, then drove back up Pacific Coast Highway, PCH, to the Kiwanis tree lot in Hermosa Beach. She'd read their banner on her drive home this morning, driving from El Segundo through Manhattan Beach and Hermosa, then to Redondo: *All Proceeds to Local Charities*. Sounded good to her.

The lot smelled like pine trees, real pine trees, not fake piped in smells. She picked out a six foot Noble fir, with nice even branches, enough room between them to showcase her ornaments, but not so much it looked skimpy. She added a tree stand and four packages of white lights; then, biting her lip, added two more packages, to string along her front porch railing. Go all out, Eliza!

One of the guys at the lot helped her get the tree, all wrapped up in the old sheet, into her front seat. She handed him a five dollar tip. "Thank you."

"Looks like you picked out a good one," someone said behind her.

She squeaked and jumped. *Way to look dignified!*

Jake smiled at her. Oh, those eyes. Spicy warm cinnamon. "Eliza, right? Want to help me pick one out for the coffee shop?" he asked. "Kathy usually helps me pick out a tree, but she's at the Bean."

The *yes* died on her lips. "I have to get my tree home," she said. "They just trimmed the end, I have to get it into the stand and water it."

Were those eyes disappointed? She didn't know. Kathy, huh?

"Well, you are coming tomorrow for game night, right? You need to get your free latte." He smiled. "I really hope you do."

She glanced up at him.

"We need all the players we can get," he continued.

Good lord. Her emotions couldn't take this. "Gotta go," she said.

"7 p.m. See you tomorrow," he said, as she hopped into the Miata and backed out.

———

Tuesday she got up early to go for a run on the Strand, the concrete path that ran the length of the Santa Monica bay, all the way from Rat Beach in Torrance (*Right After Torrance*; she finally had to ask someone why a perfectly nice beach was named after rats!) to Will Rogers State Beach out in Pacific Palisades. She'd ridden her bike along the whole forty odd miles there and back a couple times in the summer, dodging clueless tourists nearly the entire way.

There were a couple spots in Playa del Rey and Marina del Rey where the Strand wasn't continuous. The first time she rode her bike she had gotten a little lost.

She was only planning on running from her house to Hermosa Pier and back, though. Round trip that would still be about eight miles. She needed the run to burn off her lingering anger from yesterday.

And maybe she could take a break near the Pier and grab a coffee at Bean and Board. Even if there was a Kathy in the picture, she could still look, right?

And Jake made darn good coffee.

Running shorts, tank top, cap with her pony tail pulled through, and sunscreen. Lots of sunscreen. Waist belt for a water bottle, and a zipped pouch for her keys and some cash. Ready to go. She took off running at an easy clip.

Less that forty minutes later, she was breathing a bit harder and walking into the Bean.

Jake wasn't at the counter.

A woman was. Pretty, with long dark hair and warm brown eyes, and a quick smile. "Hi!" she said. "Welcome to Bean and Board. Is this your first time?"

"Um," Eliza said. This must be Kathy. Her heart sank. She was so pretty. And nice. "Second time."

"Awesome, a repeat customer!" Kathy said. "Fantastic. We must be doing something right." She grinned. "You must've met Jake last time? I'm Kathy, his big sister."

Sister!

"And I know he's super cute, but," she leaned forward on the counter top, "I make way better coffee. Don't tell him that."

"I'm coming for game night tonight," Eliza said. "That's still on, right?"

"You bet. 7 p.m. But come a little early if you want to help pick out some games. You're Eliza, right? Jake mentioned you. Can't miss that glorious hair of yours." Kathy swiped some imaginary crumbs off the counter. "But don't tell him I said that, either. Coffee?"

"Latte, please, a double. Whole milk." Eliza smiled.

This was turning into the best week *ever*.

———

6:30 p.m. and Eliza was back at Bean and Board. It was already dark out, and Jake and Kathy had Christmas lights along the roof and windows of the cottage, giving it a cheery festive glow. She could see a decorated and lit Christmas tree through the front window. The smell of cinnamon coffee cake, fresh coffee, and eggnog enveloped her as she walked up.

She was wearing a bit of makeup that accentuated her bright green eyes, and her favorite jeans that fit her snugly in all the right places, along with a navy cotton Aran sweater Dr Jacobs, Lacey, had knit for her when Eliza told her she was moving to Los Angeles. Cotton, not wool, but Lacey said it did get chilly in the evenings, from what she remembered from a long ago trip to Catalina. A thick cozy sweater would be welcome. Blue suede loafers with a rubber soul completed her outfit.

Eliza's curly red hair floofed around her face and down her back, a nimbus of cheer.

Kathy was at the counter, helping a customer, when Eliza walked in. Smiling, she gave Eliza a quick thumbs up. Eliza thought she mouthed "You go, girl!" but she wasn't sure.

Eliza waved hello, then headed back to the long table off to the left. As she expected, that was the site for game night. Jake was there, looking scrumptious in faded jeans, olive green khaki sneakers, and an atrocious ugly Christmas sweater featuring reindeer, an abominable snowman, and a Tyrannosaurus with a Santa cap. He was sorting through a stack of colorful boxes: Catan, Ticket to Ride, Pandemic, and some others she didn't recognize.

"Need help?" she asked.

"Eliza! I'm so glad you made it," Jake said, eyes lighting up.

"I needed something fun to look forward to," she said. "Lost my job yesterday."

"Oh, no," he said. "Are you okay?"

She thought for a moment. "Actually, yes, I am. I was over at Orbital, and I hated it. I should've left on my own months ago, but I thought I could make it work. I'm not used to not being able to make things work."

"So you're a rocket scientist?" he said.

She blushed. "Basically, yes." She watched him beneath her lashes. If he was going to be intimidated, it would be now.

"Awesome," he said. "I had a great Physics teacher in high school, Ms Nolan. I wish I had more aptitude for it myself. Majored in English Lit and surfing at Santa Cruz, and look where I am now."

"You're doing fine," Kathy called from the counter.

Jake rolled his eyes. "Typical pushy big sister. So where are you from originally?"

"Chicago area," she said. "Then east coast, Yale and MIT. I moved out here last spring for the job."

"Oooh, fancy," he teased. "Must've been culture shock for you, though, moving out west."

She nodded. "I miss the seasons. And I miss the snow. I used to make a snowman, each Christmas break, in my backyard in Boston." Suddenly, she could feel herself tearing up. She missed her research, Lacey, and, most of all, her parents.

"Oh, sweetheart," Jake said, walking around the table to her, gathering her up in his arms.

She tensed, then let herself relax against him, burying her face in that godawful sweater, sobbing. She hoped she didn't smear mascara on it.

With her luck she would. All over the ridiculously cheery Tyrannosaur.

He stroked her hair and murmured nonsense to her. Finally, after a long couple minutes, she straightened, dashing at her eyes. "I'm so sorry," she said.

"You don't ever have to apologize to me," he said, tilting her chin up to meet her eyes. His cinnamon eyes were soft, concerned. "But hold on. Sit here, I'll be back in a few. I'll have Kathy make you a latte. Whole milk, two shots, right?"

"Yes," she said. "Thanks." She plopped down on the bench, watching him stop to talk to Kathy briefly, then head back into the kitchen. He came out, carrying a small paper bag, with a rolled up blue and red beach towel tucked under his arm, just as Kathy finished making her latte.

"Come on," he said, handing her the latte in a to-go cup and grabbing her other hand. "Kathy will start up game night. Some friends of ours promised to show up for it, so if we're a little late, it's okay."

"Where are we going?"

"Just to the beach. I need to show you something."

———

They walked down to the hard packed sand at the ocean's edge, trudging first through the loose sand, getting grains stuck in their shoes. Eliza had to take off her suede loafers; the sand in her shoes was driving her nuts, but unfortunately that meant she had to let go of Jake's hand.

He spread the beach towel on the soft, dry sand just shy of the damp hard pack. "Give me ten minutes, okay?" he asked. She nodded, sitting back on the towel, wedging her latte into the sand next to her.

She could feel a the mist of ocean spray from the waves slapping against the shore. Tide was going out. Bioluminescent plankton colored the waves a soft aqua in the moonlight. The brininess was strong, pungent, crisp in the cool December air.

Jake was mounding up piles of wet sand into what looked like ... a snowman? A rather awkward, small, slumping snowman, about two feet tall, but yes, something that did look sort of like a snowman. He pulled two burnt cookies from the paper bag and stuck them onto the face (or, more precisely, what he must have intended to be the face) for eyes, then held out the bag to her.

"Your turn," he said.

She reached in, pulled out a carrot, and laughed. She stuck it into the sandy face, below the cookie eyes.

He reached an arm out, and she tucked back under it, against his warm body. He tentatively, gently, kissed the top of her head. "It's not exactly a snowman," he said. "But it's the best I can do on very short notice."

"It's perfect," Eliza said, her heart soaring.

All of a sudden, it did feel like Christmas.

the
MERMAID
of
ELLIS PRIME

AND SEVEN
ADDITIONAL
SCIENCE FICTION
SHORT STORIES

SCIENCE FICTION AND FANTASY AUTHOR
STEPHANNIE
TALLENT

THE MEDIC OF THE CROW CITY
MINING CO-OP

I wrote "The Medic of the Crow City Mining Co-op" at a science
fiction short story workshop.
The assignment?
Explore Springs Preserves in Las Vegas.
And come up with a short story.
In about 24 hours.
And it's my favorite story I wrote for the workshop.

———

MIRI PLACED her battered aluminum lunch tray on the empty plastiform table in the far corner of the canvas-covered crew mess area.

Everywhere was loud: good-natured shouting and guffaws from the crews, the clanks and whirs of the drilling machines, the high-pitched whine of the generators.

The corner seemed quietest.

The white table was so coated with fine dust it looked pink. She ran a finger through it. Powdery. It would get everywhere. Pores, eyes, lungs. Probably cause cancer ten years down the road, but none of the miners wore masks or respirators.

Just breathed it all in.

Sure, most cancers were curable, but cancer still sucked. No sense in complacency.

Mining crews and other workers of the Crow City Mining Co-op crowded around most of the tables in the mess area. Miri identified at least five different distinct languages that she herself spoke, and a jumble that she didn't. If she sat by herself, she could focus, block out the cacophony, acclimatize.

"Good luck," her Assignments Officer had said drily before she flew out. "Last camp medic quit within two weeks, forfeiting all her regular pay on top of the hazard bennies. Try not to piss off the bosses, this time, and I'll get you somewhere nice for the next assignment."

Promises, promises. She was beholden to the Planetary Personnel Workforce, the PPW (or Pew Pew, when she was feeling particularly grumpy), for another five years, for paying for her medical degree. She'd already served ten. She knew the score.

Miri stepped over the plastiform bench and eased herself down, stretching her long, travel-sore legs out in front of her. She'd grabbed a bowl of some sort of chowder from one of the bins in the center of the mess, not even caring what it was. Protomeat, vege, native road-kill. Who cared. Planet hopping always threw off her stomach, and the change from stale recycled ship's air to a planet side atmosphere numbed her taste buds anyway.

And this atmosphere...she could feel her lips chapping. Hot and dusty and mummifyingly dry. The shade from the canvas awning did little to cool off the mess hall, just kept the crews from blistering in the mid-day sun. The camp was centered in a narrow canyon, one of many side canyons in this maze of badlands, off the main canyon, the site of the actual mining, but the three hundred meter tall, glowing red and pink cliffs couldn't block the overhead sun.

Some enterprising soul had hung some fluid-soaked cotton sheets up as an impromptu swamp cooler, but the pungent scent wafting from them with every gust of wind made her wonder what the liquid was.

Hell, she wasn't wondering.

Someone pissed on 'em. Probably thought it was funny.

Guess there was enough water to not worry about recycling urine. Of course, the river in the main canyon was the whole bugaboo in this op, from her quick reading on the transit over. Rare minerals, river in the way, move it over and dig to high holy hell, damn the consequences to any native species.

Story of every low-tech exploited world.

No wonder she was grumpy all the time.

Five years. Just five more years.

She dipped her spoon (also bent, pitted, aluminum, must be cheap, here) into the chowder. Took a taste.

Spat it out and grabbed her water canteen, knowing the water would just push the vicious heat closer to her tongue but needing to do *something*.

High holy fuck, what the hell did they put in there? Some native pepper ten times hotter than a freakin' ghost chili?

"Doc! Hey, DOC!"

Miri kept her watering eyes downcast. God, no. Just no.

"Doc! Who'd you piss off, to get posted here?" Jimmy Two Dogs plopped on the bench across from here, all two meters tall and hundred fifty kilos of him. His long red hair was pulled back in a stringy ponytail. Dirt creased the lines in his tanned face, aging him thirty years. "Long time no see!"

Not long enough. She'd met Jimmy Two Dogs four years ago. 0935-Orion, asteroid mining operation. A one year assignment that had felt like ten.

She got in trouble *there* when she joined with the striking miners. Jimmy Two Dogs had been their leader.

What else was she supposed to do? The miners were her friends, and they were dying because of fucking cheap ass faulty bichlorbutylene explosives and other piece-of-crap, lowest-bidder equipment.

Jimmy Two Dogs was a great guy.

Just really, really loud.

And who had she pissed off, this last time? Who *hadn't* she? She'd run out of fingers and toes if she tried to count them all, and space travel had gifted Miri's momma with a mutation that gave her daughter Miri six dexterous fingers on each hand.

"Hey, Jimmy. Keeping out of trouble?"

"What do you think, Doc? I'm here, ain't I?" He laughed loudly, then started hacking, pulling up big globs of rosy dust-streaked phlegm. "Lots of work for ya here, Doc. Lots of work. The mother fucking dust on top a the routine crap dealin' with this much blasting and pouring."

His dark eyes grew serious. "And the Yappers. Some accidents...they just ain't normal. The Yappers have something to do with the problems here. The guys know it, the bosses won't admit it. You watch out, Doc."

"The Yappers?"

"Little foxy natives. Regits, they call themselves. Cute as fuck, but nasty tempers. Poisonous fangs like a viper. Yap like the coyotes back home. Yappers." He leaned back, eyed her bowl. "You ain't gonna eat that stew, are ya? Let me take it off your hands. Go get some of the yellow stuff. Better for prissy white gals like you. Won't set your gut on fire."

"Yeah, yeah," Miri muttered. Who the fuck was he calling prissy? Jimmy Two Dogs had more curves than she did, with her nearly two meter tall, leanly muscled body. And yeah, she kept her curly, gray-streaked brown hair long, but that was just because it was easier to pin it up in a messy bun than get it trimmed all the time.

She passed him her stew. She wasn't hungry anyway.

What the fuck had she gotten herself into this time?

———

The clinic was more poorly stocked than she'd anticipated. And it wasn't like she was an optimistic, glass half full kind of gal.

Two modified shipping containers, insulated and air conditioned, thank the gods, formed the clinic. It had running water and electricity. She shouldn't have to note that, but she'd actually reported once to a unit that lacked those amenities.

The irregular hum and creaks of the air conditioner suggested it needed a tune up. Add that to the list.

One container included a small sterile surgery suite in the center. A stasis storage room was adjacent to the surgery suite, with five coffin-like padded support boxes for patients who needed shipment off-world to a full medical facility. All were currently empty. On the opposite end of the container was a non-sterile treatment room, with two patient treatment stations.

The other container had an examination room, two storage rooms with chipped plastiwood cabinetry lining the walls, and a small room at the end far end she could use as living quarters. It contained a stripped twin mattress on a simple aluminum bed frame and the plastiform desk and chair. An ancient comms terminal took up most of the desk, with a dusty monitor and a small detached keyboard.

A small ultrasonic shower and a narrow closet with a few bent hangers hanging off an aluminum clothes bar filled the back wall. A small plastiwood cabinet, storage for personal items, sat under the aluminum clothes bar. Neatly folded, but dusty, sheets and a lumpy pillow sat on top of the cabinet.

She'd eat in the mess. Take a water-based shower once a week, rely on the ultrasonic for day to day.

That made the set up better than some of the posts she'd drawn.

But beyond the physical layout...when she started opening storage cabinets, all she found was dust. Pink dust, despite the negative air flow integrated into the air system, that should have kept the dust out. The whole clinic smelled of the faint sulfur, like the cliffs.

Like this whole damn planet, far as she could tell.

Well, at least she didn't have a lot of crap she couldn't use taking up space.

She finally found one cabinet that had some supplies. A couple bottles of antibiotics, some pain control patches, a couple bottles of anesthetics for the inhalant anesthetic machine, a couple boxes of sterile bandaging material.

She made a mental list of everything she'd need to order. She expected the site had a lot of physical trauma injuries. More antibiotics, pain management, anesthetics. Wound care materials, bandaging supplies, casting supplies. She doubted the Co-op would spring for an on-site regenerator, or a quick healing unit, or a full body scanner, but she could ask. It was probably cheaper to hire new workers and ship off the old broken ones than maintain high tech medical equipment.

This felt more like a forward triage set up than a permanent clinic.

That meant people would die, had been dying, even with the stasis units, if it was as bad as Jimmy Two Dogs said.

She'd do her best. That's all she could do.

All she ever did.

She headed towards the Co-op on-site headquarters, slogging through the pink sand, keeping to the shade of the sheer canyon walls. First thing: discuss (yeah, that was the term she wanted, not *order*, not *demand*) what she needed for the clinic. Second, find out how many nurses and assistants she had floating around (she suspected the number was zero). Oh, and to introduce herself like a proper professional to the camp commander, Brugart. Can't forget that.

The concussive force of an explosion punched her in the gut.

Then screams, echoing, bouncing, off the maze of canyon walls. Human screams.

And a shrill yipping, barking. Yapping.

She could also hear, or sense, a low thrumming shriek, that made her ears ache, so much she clapped her hands over her ears and pressed just to make it stop.

The cliff sides were vibrating.

Fist-sized jagged red and peach rocks, studded with pink crystals, broke free from the cliffs and tumbled down, the crystals ringing as they impacted the cliff side, shaking more dust into the air. Miri slogged through the sand to the center of the canyon, heedless of the blistering sunlight, heedless of the crowd of workers spilling like ants out of the mess tent, HQ, and the nearby recreation and living tents.

Last thing she needed was to get killed by a rock on her first day. "What the *fuck*," she said, coughing. The pink dust filled her mouth, burning with sharp stabs of sulfur.

Which way? She couldn't tell, with everyone shoving and running and yelling.

A plume of pink dust mushroomed overhead in the seconds it took it to clear the canyon walls.

Someone grabbed her arm, began dragging her down canyon. Towards the main operation. Towards the site of the explosion.

Handed her a water-soaked kerchief that she tied over her mouth. Her coughing eased.

Jimmy Two Dogs, his dark eyes anxious.

"Come on, Doc!" he urged. "Those guys are gonna need you!"

They ran.

Triage mode.

Broken arms, broken legs, broken ribs. They could wait. Don't listen to the screams. Skull crushed. Three of those. Sorry, guys. Torn off limbs, ripped open guts. Ignore the reek of leaking feces, the acrid stench of burning chlorine, rubber and plastic from the explosives.

Too late for him, him, and that one—but her, she might make it.

Jimmy tied a tourniquet, using his size triple X overshirt, at Miri's direction, high up on the stump of the woman's leg. The arterial spurting slowed, stopped.

Gods above, what Miri wouldn't do for a regenerator. Or a couple dozen more stasis units.

As Miri walked amongst the body parts and blood and jagged rocks and the mist of blowing dust, an Angel of Death in a lightweight rip stop camo jumpsuit passing judgment, Jimmy yelled and hustled and organized a crew to follow her orders.

Turn him over—aw, shit, never mind. Back of the head gone.

And that was that. At least thirty dead, and a few more she knew wouldn't even make it to the stasis boxes. No regenerator and dozens who needed one ASAP.

And there, at the edge of the debris, a small furry form, maybe a meter long, a meter and a half if you included the bushy tail. Pricked ears, a black button nose at the end of a delicate pointed snout, sharp pointed teeth that she bet were the venomous fangs, and plush dusty gray fur, like a little fox. Its eyes, either side of that little snout, were tightly shut.

It curled in on itself, dark blue blood leaking from somewhere under its body, pooling under it and staining the loose linen tunic it wore purple.

Its blood smelled like sugary copper, even in the sulfur and rubber explosive haze.

A Regit. Native sentient species. What Jimmy and everyone else called a Yapper.

There was something else to that smell...not the Regit, who smelled better than most dogs she'd met, but the explosives...that chlorine, rubbery smell....

The Regit opened its eyes, huge indigo eyes with a star-shaped pupil. Stared at her fearlessly.

Reached out one delicate, clawed hand.

Miri bent down and reached back, grasped the little hand gently. The Regit's hand was so small it only took four of her six fingers, to hold it.

She had no freaking idea how to treat a Yapper. Regit. A *Regit*.

Call it by its chosen species name, not some derogatory term.

And treatment? *Common sense, girl. Use your head.*

"Are you alright—" she started, even as she visually assessed the Yap—*Regit*. Steady breathing, the pool of blood was—*was it actually receding? was the Regit actually resorbing it? —wow, that was so freaking cool!*

The indigo eyes grew brighter and the grip on her fingers stronger.

"Aid, help, assist," the Regit said, its voice high pitched and breathy.

"I will," Miri promised. She didn't know if it was in pain or if always squeaked. No wonder the Co-op dismissed the Regits. Tiny, cute, fluffy creature, it looked more like a stuffed toy than a sentient being.

All she knew, she had to help it.

"Take that creature into custody."

Miri stood and turned. Her eyes flicked to the nametag on the man's camo jumpsuit. M.A. Brugart. Lovely. The camp commander. What a way to meet him.

Brugart was a beefy man, with bulging biceps and thighs stretching out the fabric of his uniform. Narrow pale brown eyes over chiseled cheekbones. A raised, jagged scar bisected his left eyebrow and trailed around his left eye, pulling the outer corner of his lids down, skewing his regular features. The scar dribbled out on his cheek. His salt and pepper hair was buzzed in a high and tight cut, so short that she bet his head was perpetually sunburnt.

Someone was living out their military fantasies.

"Nope, sorry, it's my patient," Miri said. "Article 15b, paragraph 66a. Anyone under the care of official medical staff remains there until released by the doctor in charge.

"Me."

Fuck you, you jumped up 'roided out autocrat.

"Shouldn't you be doing something to figure out what happened here?" Miri added.

He purpled. Miri marveled. She'd never seen anyone ever do that before. 'Least not someone not strangled.

"Should I add blood pressure meds to my list of requested supplies?" She bent down and scooped up the Regit. It weighed less than twenty kilos. Its tunic made a soft clacking noise; she hadn't noticed earlier, but the tunic primarily consisted of pockets, stuffed with all sorts of things. Rocks, chunks of wood, who knew what else. Made sense. A furred being wouldn't need clothing in this sort of climate, but everyone used pockets.

Up close, the Regit's sugar sweet smell was even stronger, with an underscent of vanilla musk.

"Get out of my sight," Brugart said, his voice low. "I know what happened here. Those animals blew up my mining operation. Just get the fuck out of my site. And if that creature escapes, it's on you."

———

Miri carried the Regit back to her clinic, cradled against her chest. Jimmy Two Dogs, bless him, had organized a small crew of workers to clean off the mess tables and lay out the less injured victims.

They'd laid out dead behind the mess tent, away from her clinic.

Someone had yanked down the urine soaked sheets cooling the mess tent and covered the rows of bodies. Miri knew no disrespect was intended. The sheets were handy, and the survivors didn't need to see their mangled dead friends. And anyone who had thought it was funny to piss on the sheets, instead of taking the sheets to the water buffalo, a truck with a water tank, and soaking them there with actual *water* out of the *water* storage truck, was either sorry or dead themselves.

"Hey, Doc," Jimmy Two Dogs said, as she quickly surveyed the victims. He'd done a good job.

"Hey, Jimmy. Worst cases off in the clinic?" she asked.

"Yeah. I rounded up some guys who'd done field medicine before. They got some IV lines going, some morphine, in the worst of 'em. Doc, we don't got enough supplies."

"I know, Jimmy. I'll figure out something."

"Doc, watch yourself," he said, nodding at the Regit in her arms. "That little guy isn't going to be very popular around here."

"The Regits didn't set off the explosion, Jimmy. Did you smell the bichlorbutylene?" That chlorinated rubber smell. Last time she smelled it was on 0935-Orion.

When *that* mining company bought cheap ass explosives and killed two hundred miners.

Things never changed.

Jimmy Two Dog's eyes widened.

"Holy shit, Doc. Fuck. You're right. Something always, uh, stank about this op." He winced. "Sorry."

"I got work to do, Jimmy. But tonight, let's you and I meet up. I need to see the plans for this operation. I'm hoping you can help me retrieve them."

———

She jury-rigged the stasis boxes to hold two people each. Jimmy Two Dogs kept referring to the guys, but in reality, half the miners and workers were female.

If she stacked a smaller person, male or female, with a larger (usually) male, she got twice the use out of each box.

And potentially saved five lives.

She lost half a dozen regardless. And a couple more might not make it.

Jimmy had found some good help for her, but she was short ten operating rooms, twenty surgeons, and twice that many nurses and techs, and who knew how much in supplies, meds and materials.

She did the best she could.

She'd let the little Yapper—the *Regit*—curl up on her bunk. It—he—seemed like he just needed rest and time to heal. Remarkable being.

By the time she'd finished in the clinic, it was nearly dawn. She wouldn't have much time to break into HQ, look for the reports she needed to find.

She met Jimmy Two Dogs just outside the clinic. The camp was quiet. The winds that had blown dust everywhere early had stopped, and the air was clear, free of dust. And it was freaking cold. Goose-bumps pimpled her arms.

The cliffs glittered in the glow of moonlight. Three moons, she remembered, but only one was up the sky, a sharp crescent against the velvet dark sky straight overhead. This deep in the canyon, she couldn't see any hint of dawn.

Sugar spun vanilla tickled her nose. The Regit stood beside her. His star-shaped pupils had dilated in the darkness, making his eyes look like black sapphire crystalline canyons.

A second person waited with Jimmy, dwarfed by his bulk.

"Hey, Doc," Jimmy said. "This is J.B. They hack for fun. Figured we needed to get in and out pretty damn quick, so we could use a bit of help."

Miri looked at J.B., who stared at the ground and kicked at a red rock. Average body, straight shoulder length dark hair, a symmetrical but otherwise forgettable face. They'd be ignored wherever they went. Useful, that.

"Okay, thanks," Miri said.

The four of them walked to headquarters, Miri warming up with the exertion of slogging through the soft sand. The Regit, graceful and light, walked upright, silent except for the soft clonk of items in his pockets.

"What do you carry?" Miri asked.

The Regit glanced at her, then reached into one pocket, stopped, then another. He withdraw a small flat chunk of pale wood, only a couple centimeters across, and handed it to her. It was carved with deep spirals on both sides. She rubbed her fingers over it. Otherwise smooth, sanded, no splinters. Pretty, but....

She handed it back. "It's lovely."

He refused it. "Smell," he said, his voice fluting.

She raised it to her nose. Cinnamon? The Regit motioned for her to move the chunk. She did, sniffing along it. Cinnamon segued to something deeper, richer, maybe bittersweet chocolate but she couldn't quite tell. And then, the scent changed once more, as she turned it over and smelled the other side, to a brown sugary sweet-ness, brown sugar and something nutty.

Art. It was a piece of art. The scent was imbued into the spiral carvings.

"I want dessert," she said, and the Regit smiled, pink tongue lolling.

"Keep it," he said in his breathy voice. She wondered how much she was missing, with her human nose, how many layers she just couldn't sense.

"Thank you," she said.

They reached HQ. It was the most permanent-appearing building in the camp, a simple pre-fab structure of insulated plasti-wood and dust-etched plexi windows. It was big enough for half a dozen small offices, nothing more.

J.B. did something to the scanner and the door slid open. Quieter and more efficient than Miri's first thought, which was to bash in one of the windows, if it had just been her and Jimmy Two Dogs.

They entered the building into a center hallway that stretched the length of the building. Closed doors lined either side of the hall-way. It was dark and quiet, except for their boots scuffing on the dusty gray plastitile floor.

Empty.

"Engineers are working out of that room," Jimmy said, gesturing to the second door on the right. J.B. did their magic again, and they entered.

The room was windowless, the air inside still. Miri flicked the light switch, turning on overhead lights that lit the room with a pale buttery glow. Dessert on the brain.

Two plastiform desks with high tech terminals sat in the center of the room. One entire wall was an interactive glass screen, displaying a map of the canyonlands, the course of the river....and what was marked as a Regit settlement, downriver, near where the river spread into an estuary by an ocean.

"Work's going slow," J.B. said, speaking for the first time, her voice raspy. "Regs. Have to measure impact on natives, on the Regits, before doing anything major."

"Article 45b." *Any exploitation of natural resources must be thoroughly evaluated for impact on the environment and any native species, and reassessed after each adjustment.* Miri tapped the screen. The view shifted, highlighting the mineral deposits deep under the canyons. Deep under the river.

"If the Regits weren't there, it would be easier to mine all that. And cheaper." J.B. said. "Move the river, blast everything, instead of the targeted excavations we've been doing."

"You've thought about this," Miri said.

J.B. shrugged. "Same thing happened on my home world. Happens all the time."

Miri couldn't argue with that.

"And if the Yap—the Regit were shown to be dangerous, the Co-op could fight back," Jimmy said. "Like if they were setting off bombs, to get us to leave."

The Regit yipped. "Tried to stop it," he said. "Tried."

Miri heard a soft swoosh. The front door. "Guys—"

The hall lights flickered on. Heavy steps, boots on the plastitile floor, not trying to be quiet.

Brugart.

"Well," he said, filling the doorway. "Well. I'm not surprised to see you all here."

"Brugart, your operation is in direct contradiction to Article 45b. And I'm sure we'll find actual evidence that you caused today's incident, resulting in the deaths of thirty employees, and you will be charged with—"

"Doc, shut the fuck up," Brugart said.

The Regit apparently decided enough was enough.

He ran to, and *up*, Brugart, using his fine claws to climb up Brugart like a kitten climbing curtains.

And he bit Brugart on the nose.

Brugart fell like a rock, foam dribbling between his lips, the Regit leaping clear.

"Not dead," the Regit said, with a bit of regret in his voice. "But will stay unconscious, for as long as needed. Collect your evidence, please."

———

It wasn't quite that easy. J.B. had to hack into the systems, and pull together a coherent report from all the hidden, filed away data, orders, and so on.

The Regit left, then returned with small contingency of Regits, who assisted J.B., using the maps to communicate their knowledge of their world, the destruction the operation would cause.

J.B. hacked into the comms and got that report distributed. Not just to the higher ups at Crow City Mining Co-op, but to the Interplanetary Law and Justice Agency, the ILJA.

And the news services.

Jimmy Two Dogs hunted down the bichlorbutylene explosives. Not faulty, this time, just not something the Regit could ever have accessed. Not something commonly used. Miri could never forget that acrid chlorine smell, after 0935-Orion.

Miri herself had the distasteful task of making sure Brugart didn't just die, on top of caring for all the injured workers. She stored Brugart's rigid body with the stasis boxes and assigned a watch on him. Check his vitals every three hours, clean him up so he wouldn't get bed sores, and so on. He wasn't worth any more of her time, than that.

The Regit's venom induced stasis. Nifty. Could be useful, if she could analyze it then synthesize it.

That afternoon, a shuttle arrived with a complete medical team.

And a team of military police and investigators.

————

Two weeks later.

Miri lay on a blue towel, on a pink sand beach, the hot sun high overhead, just a floppy straw hat shading her face. The gentle lap of waves against the sand lulled her, as did the fluting voices of the juvenile Regit splashing in the bay.

Jimmy Two Dogs plopped down next to her, kicking up a dusting of sand.

"Dude, put some sunscreen on," she said, shading her eyes and looking at the sunburn reddening Jimmy's pale brown belly.

"Enjoying your day of R&R?" Jimmy said. "Isn't this great? The sun, the beach."

"It is," she agreed.

"The mining op is closing for good," he said. "Just heard from J.B."

"For the best," Miri said.

"The ILJA is working with the local Regit. They may set up some sort of cultural exchange. The Regit seem open to it. Crow City had everyone at ILJA convinced the Regit were just animals."

"They're sure cute," Miri said. "Easy to assume, when you don't want to look any deeper." She was learning the Regit had an incredible culture, filled with art. Stories. Scent-based sciences.

"You gonna stay?"

"I'd like to," Miri said. "For a bit of time, at least. My AO said my tour was for a year. So I'll be staying that long. Even if there's no mining, there will be a settlement, for the delegation to the Regit."

Sure, the Regit buildings and infrastructure didn't look like much.

But they smelled incredible.

the CHRONICLES of
DINAH LEE WRIGHT
Volume One
TALES OF AN
Old West
SORCERESS
STEPHANNIE
TALLENT
weird west, fantasy, & science fiction author

THE FOX SORCERER

Although the landscape of my heart is the cool waves and brilliant sunsets of the Pacific, there's a bit of the desert in my soul.
Dinah Lee Wright, a young sorceress, travels through a late 1800s American Southwest where magic and gods intertwine with the landscape.
Find more Dinah stories in The Chronicles of Dinah Lee Wright, *Volumes 1 and 2.*

———

DINAH BLINKED.

The Chinese man was still there, strolling down the muddy, wheel-rutted Main Street of West Jordan, jewel-encrusted crimson silk robe glittering in the hot early afternoon August sun.

Steam from the mud puddles licked around the Chinese man's cream leather boots and the hem of his robe, but not a spot of mud dared to mar either boots or robe.

The sleeves of his robe draped over his hands, but Dinah bet his hands were soft and his nails manicured. His long narrow queue danced around his shoulders like a string to a kite being tossed by a breeze. That same soft wind blew the scents of sage, mint, and chrysanthemum tea towards her.

His cheekbones were sharp as knives, his black eyes glinting and prideful. He looked like a prince in the prime of life, something out of a fairy tale Dinah's mama had told her when Dinah was just a child. When Dinah was content and safe and loved, with her mama and papa. 'Stead of always on edge, wondering if she could earn enough for a meal after paying for her mule Malyu's feed.

Two uncanny sandy-colored foxes gamboled behind the Chinese man, their pale paws as pristine as his boots. Spirit foxes, in material form. One glanced at her, tongue lolling in a vulpine smirk, white teeth gleaming, as it—he— bounced along. The smaller fox yipped and barked, amber eyes flashing as she glanced at Dinah.

No one else reacted. 'Course, there weren't many people out in the late summer monsoon mugginess.

The next block over, the young black hostler, Jimmy, led a fine little black-and-white paint mare to the livery behind the town's single boarding house. That little mare would join Malyu, tucked away with fresh hay.

Dinah liked Jimmy. He'd slipped Malyu a treat of sweet oats the night before, and laid out fresh hay for Dinah to sleep on.

Closer to, Mrs McKinney, pale pretty face pinched and dour in the shade of her bonnet, left the two-story general store with a basket of apples and a small roll of lace ribbon, gingham skirts swishing along.

And heading right towards Dinah and the Chinese man, Deputy Batson strolled down the street to the adobe building that served as his office and jail, touching his fingers to his felted wool fedora as he passed Mrs. McKinney. Mrs. McKinney nodded to him, but her eyes skated right past Dinah's when she walked by Dinah. To her, Dinah was lower than the fat ruby-carapaced dung beetles rolling around in the street near the horse droppings, and not near as pretty.

'Course Deputy Batson didn't bother tipping his hat to Dinah, neither. He tolerated her, but that was it.

Not a one even seemed to see the Chinese man and his foxes.

Dinah trusted her instincts. And her instincts were screaming that if no one else saw this man strolling down the center of Main Street, brazen as a snake oil salesman , like he owned every last building and every single person in town, she ought to pretend she couldn't see him either. She knew, better than most, the prejudice against Chinese, being herself the daughter of a Chinese prostitute.

But she doubted someone so proud and aristocratic would hide his presence, unless he had a nefarious purpose.

She could discover that purpose later. Right now, she slunk back into the narrow shaded passageway between the saloon and boarding house, ignoring the pungent stink of piss. Luckily, she dressed like a boy: blunt toed leather boots, heavy canvas pants, and a loose-fitting shirt with a wool vest to hide her slim figure. No long skirts to drag in the muck.

Her long glossy hair was tied up in a loose bun off her neck, tucked up under a black wool felt hat. Sweat traced a warm wet trail down her spine.

Dinah hoped the Chinese sorcerer (for what else could he be, with those two fox spirits?) didn't catch a taste of her own small, lonely magics on the breeze.

She bit at a hangnail, drawing a rusty-tasting drop of blood that she smeared on the silver look-away charm she wore on a leather lace around her neck.

It seemed to work. Least-wise no fox or sorcerer turned down the passageway to confront her. Rather, they continued right on down the street, those foxes yapping as they pounced after grasshoppers coming to take sips of the rain puddles.

Dinah reckoned herself a cautious woman. As a bounty hunting, problem-solving, half-Chinese sorceress for hire, driven by her need for justice in a land that served little, aided by her own magics inherited from her mama, she had to be cunning and prudent and wary.

Not someone who'd let curiosity gnaw at her belly til she left that passageway to follow the sorcerer.

But that's what Dinah did.

———

The Chinese sorcerer set up camp a couple miles out of the far side of town, in the clearing under the desert willow trees that encircled the spring feeding Scott's Creek, the source of West Jordan's sweet water supply. Thick chaparral, snowberry, and juniper grew intermixed with the trees on either side of the trail leading up to the spring.

Dinah didn't take the trail.

She circled 'round to the far side of the spring, then laid down and crawled on her belly through the needle grass, under and around the scrub and rocks, til she found a suitable spot tucked behind a dreamy willow. She could see the sorcerer and still be downwind from those foxes. Aromatic creosote, piney and lemony, flavored the muggy air. She hoped it would help cover the stench of her sweat.

One fox lounged on a plush red rug in front of a small cream-colored silk tent. The tent was four feet tall, just big enough to give shelter to a thick pile of embroidered blankets and silk pillows.

The other fox lapped water from the clear spring, then dabbed a paw in, likely trying for a trout or crawdad.

The sorcerer tended a small ornate brass brazier, feeding it dried sticks and herbs. His over-robe hung from a branch, leaving him in heavy draping silk trousers and a woven linen shirt, the latter sheer in the leaf-dappled sunlight, showing off a mighty fine torso.

A wisp of sage-scented smoke wafted towards Dinah's hiding place, tickling her nose and watering her eyes. She kept staring, though, til she sneezed. Couldn't help herself.

The sneezing or the staring.

He didn't even look up, just kept feeding the brazier. "You might as well come over here," he said, his voice smooth as his silk trousers that outlined everything. Everything.

Dinah wasn't the sort to be distracted by matters of the flesh. No, she was not. No matter how pretty that flesh was. No matter how lonely she was.

The sorcerer smiled, a soft quirk of his upper lip, and added more herbs. Mint joined the sage, and Dinah parted her lips with the thought of how the sorcerer must taste, bright and fresh and sweet, those finely shaped lips of his against hers.

She knew some folks who were obsessed with earthly pleasures. Men who'd gambled away their ranches and cattle to try to win the attention of a woman, women who'd left their families to be in the arms of a scoundrel. She'd never understood it before. She'd seen the physical scars her mama bore, from before meeting Dinah's father, from clients savage with lust, and recognized the emotional scars that only her papa had healed.

Dinah didn't trust the idea of physical passion, and she was glad she herself had never desired anyone before. She was alone. By choice.

But now, a pulsing ached between her legs, a desperate need to go over to him, run her hands against that heavy silk of his trousers, even smooth her hands up under that linen shirt, stroking that muscled belly.

The sorcerer sprinkled fragments of dried yellow petals over the brazier. The scent of tea, invigorating and sharp, made her whole body tingle like it never had before.

The fox on the rug yipped and rolled over, waving those cute little dipped-in-cream paws in the air, brown eyes bright.

The fox that had been drinking from the spring shook itself off and trotted to the sorcerer, weaving around and between his legs like a big friendly tom cat.

Jealousy stabbed her. Why should that creature touch him, and not her?

"Come, do not fight it," cajoled the sorcerer.

And Dinah couldn't. Couldn't resist. Didn't even want to, anymore. She rose to her knees.

Mrs. McKinney appeared from behind one of the desert willows next to the trail, opposite to Dinah's hiding spot. Her blue gingham skirt was all stained with leaves and trail muck.

She walked right up to the sorcerer and sank into his arms with a sigh that turned to a deep throated moan, rubbing herself against him like a barn cat in heat.

Dinah gaped, her mind suddenly sharp, an icy chill running through her core.

She fumbled in her bag of charms hanging from her belt, finding the brass-plated mountain lion tooth charm. A charm for protection. She grabbed her knife out of its scabbard next to the charm bag and sliced the meat at the base of her left thumb, coating the charm with her blood, turning that brass into a stormfront sunset.

Dinah hoped the charm would be powerful enough.

The sorcerer quirked a fine eyebrow at Dinah's hiding place as he lowered his lips to Mrs. McKinney's and wrapped his lean muscled arms around her.

He kissed Mrs. McKinney hard, not even letting up for a breath until Mrs. McKinney swooned, then kept kissing her, til her face sunk in and her skin dried up and flaked away, til he was holding nothing but what looked like a rat caught up somewhere it couldn't get out, and it was three months later, all papery skin and brittle bones.

The little foxes danced around the two of them all the while, yipping and waving their bushy tails around as he sucked the life force out of Mrs. McKinney.

The sorcerer dropped what was left of Mrs. McKinney and stretched his arms to the sky in satisfaction. His heavy trousers were damp in the front.

Dinah figured he'd had a mighty good time, killing Mrs. McKinney.

Dinah wasn't ignorant. Just usually uninterested.

"Come out, come out," the sorcerer crooned, his voice trying to sneak through the charm's protections.

"I don't want any of what you're offering," Dinah called back.

Nonetheless, she left her place behind the willow tree and stopped a few yards away from the sorcerer. She kept that brazier of his, still smoking tea and mint and sage, between the two of them.

She glanced at what remained of Mrs. McKinney. The larger fox, the male, was pawing at her gingham dress and shredding off bits of blue-checked fabric, tossing them in the air, batting at them. That seemed to bore him after a few moments, and he started digging and tearing through a sleeve til he got an arm bone. He settled down and began gnawing on it. It cracked like a gunshot when the fox broke it in two.

The other fox, the littler one, sat by the sorcerer's side, her amber eyes glinting in sly foxy amusement.

"What about," the sorcerer said, "the power to control the storms?" A shadow dashed over the clearing.

Dinah looked up straight overhead. Sure enough, monsoon storm clouds were roiling in, thunderheads heavy and dark with the devastating potential to cause floods and wildfires. Lightning itched at her palms, longing to be set free.

Her lion's-tooth charm flared, a spot of grounding heat against her left palm.

"The power to make those townspeople respect you, despite your birth. Despite the foreign cast to your features."

The charm burned hotter.

"Do you know what she was thinking, your Mrs. McKinney? What she feared?" he said softly. "Her foremost thought was not that she was dying. Rather, she couldn't face herself being willingly despoiled by a Chinaman.

"That's what they think of you, even when they hire you to hunt down their missing cattle, or discover who is cheating them, or whatever of the dozens of menial tasks they have you do. That you're nothing but occasionally useful trash."

Power. Power to never fear anyone again, power to give herself a life of luxury, power to be safe. Power to force folks to meet her eyes as an equal, not some bit of filth.

People killed each other for power.

Dinah didn't like to kill. She certainly did not like other folks trying to kill her.

She shook her head. "I don't want them to fear me, and that's all you're truly offering."

And she'd never, ever be safe. Always on guard, til someone managed to slit her throat out of fear or covetousness.

The charm cooled in her hand.

The storm clouds scudded away, taking away the lightning that wanted to nestle inside her.

The sorcerer gazed at Dinah, eyes narrowing, calculating. He quirked an eyebrow, kneeled to pat the little fox's head, then stood.

"So. Neither lust, nor power, is enough for you. Huli Fang," he said "go to her."

The little fox Huli Fang trotted over to Dinah and raised one creamy paw up to her.

"You are lonely," the sorcerer said. "I offer you Huli Fang. She will be your lifelong companion, always loving you, never leaving you. Your most trusted confident, the other half of your heart."

The charm burned so hot Dinah dropped it.

It exploded before it hit the ground, fragments of molten brass and ivory tooth flashing like stars. Some brass splattered on her left hand, scorching it, and she wiped her hand against her trousers furiously, tears streaming down her cheeks.

A chasm of loneliness, deep and lost, lay open and uncovered in her heart. Dinah knew it was truly there. All her life, since her mama and papa died, she'd been covering that hole with learning and travelling and work. Always alone, not fitting in with her papa's fancy people back East, who were aghast he'd settled with a Chinese woman. Never fitting in with the Chinese here, her mama a prostitute, lowest of the low.

That oubliette of misery and loneliness had grown deeper and deeper over the years, like an abandoned mine shaft being eaten away by an underground river.

Didn't matter that the charm was destroyed. It never could protect against this.

Dinah stroked Huli Fang's soft head. Like silk, her fur was. The fox licked her burnt hand, cooling it.

Dinah took one step, two, three towards the sorcerer. Mint and tea and sage swirled around her. Huli Fang walked with her, pressing her warm furry body close against Dinah's leg.

His handsome face relaxed, and she held out her burnt left hand to him. He took it, drawing her to him. His warm touch soothed the burns on her hand. His black eyes, amused and intrigued, met hers.

He smiled at her, and Dinah smiled right back.

She stabbed him in the heart with the knife held in her right hand. Aimed between his ribs, slipping in like a freshwater eel amongst the marsh grass.

He pushed her away, stumbling against the brazier, knocking it over, scattering the remaining bits of herbs and leaves. Dark crimson heart's blood drenched that fine linen shirt of his, molding it to his torso. The storm clouds rushed across the sky, and lightning struck a desert willow across the spring. Torrential rain doused any burning bits left over from the brazier.

Hail stones the size of peas pelted Dinah, the bite of each icy stone bringing her back to herself.

He fell, gasping, a bewildered look in his eyes. It didn't take long for him to die, those black pupils dilating, the wide deep darkness echoing the chasm in her heart. His handsome face, so smooth and pretty, dried up til he looked like what was left of Mrs. McKinney: a husk devoid of any remnant of life.

The hail stopped and the rain petered out.

The foxes, Huli Fang and her mate, their fur matted and soaked, stood stock still, gaping at her, jaws loose.

"Git," she said, dry-eyed, mopping rain from her brow. "I don't want you anyways."

———

Dinah hiked back to town, carrying a makeshift bundle made of the sorcerer's tent, filled with his charms and other sorcerous paraphernalia. She'd study it all later, when she reached a safe spot away from West Jordan.

Dinah couldn't stay in West Jordan. She needed to pack up her mule, Malyu, and leave. Mrs. McKinney was going to be missed, if she wasn't already, and who better to blame than the half Chinese girl who tried to pass as a boy, and studied and used dark magics to boot?

Dinah didn't relish the thought of a noose around her neck. She'd seen that happen to enough people she knew were innocent, but whose foreign features or dark skin condemned them despite any inconvenient truths.

The foxes had run away after she rejected them. She couldn't forget seeing the male fox chewing on Mrs. McKinney's arm bone, sucking out the last bits of marrow. If they had minds enough to choose her, Dinah, (and that's the only way she'd have one as a companion), they had minds enough to have chosen the sorcerer and partaken in his wickedness.

That she couldn't abide.

She sorrowed for Mrs. McKinney, that sad weak woman, even though Mrs. McKinney wouldn't have thought twice about her. Or once, for that matter.

Sorrowed even more for the heady crazy rush of riding the storm clouds blowing across the sky, lightning in her hands.

Sorrowed about that chasm of loneliness, plunging deep into her heart, unfilled.

But she wasn't sorry for herself.

ABOUT THE AUTHOR

Since graduating from West Point, Stephannie Tallent has served in the Army as a Military Intelligence officer during Desert Storm, gotten a Zoology degree, went to vet school, worked as a small animal veterinarian, and designed and published knitting patterns and books.

Throughout all that she's always wanted to be a writer, and she's finally put all her type A, soft-spoken, invisible middle-aged woman focus on that goal, writing everything from fantasy to science fiction, mysteries and romance.

She has sold stories to **Pulphouse Magazine** and the **WMG Holiday Spectacular**.

www.stephannietallent.com

Sign up for Stephannie's newsletter!
https://www.stephannietallent.com/subscribe/

ALSO BY STEPHANNIE TALLENT

Short Story Collections

Gates of Wonder

The Chronicles of Dinah Lee Wright Vol 1

The Chronicles of Dinah Lee Wright Vol 2

Gratitude of the Ocean: Jolene Tomberlin Series

The Serpent in the Shallows: Jolene Tomberlin Series

The Monkey's Journal

The Kaleidoscope Jaguars of the Jungles of Mexicatl

The Mermaid of Ellis Prime

One Plus One Equals More (mystery/crime)

A Snowman Made of Sand (romance)

KnitWitch (fantasy and knitting patterns)